Library of Congress Control Number: 2021907100

To my parents, my biggest
supporters in life, thank you.
        -Ariana

To Roxy- there's no greater love
than the love of a dog.
        -Paige

Roxy and Velvet's Big Adventure
Written by Ariana Pelosci
Illustrated by Paige Kelly

It was a warm and sunny summer morning and Velvet, the fluffy black cat, was asleep on her deck. This was her favorite place to be when down at the beach.

Suddenly, the door to the house next to hers squeaked open, and her very best friend Roxy, the energetic black dog, came skidding out.

WIPE YOUR PAWS

"Velvet, Velvet! Are you awake?" Roxy asked while jumping up and down tryin to see her friend.

"If I wasn't before, I am now," Velvet replied.

Velvet walked towards the gate that separated her and Roxy. "I'm so bored here," Roxy complained. "My human always leaves me for hours at a time to go to the beach. I want to go explore."

"Where are we going to go?" Velvet asked. "There are too many people here and my owner would be so sad if I left."

"We won't be gone long. They won't even notice that we left!" She began to jump up and down, trying to open the latch on th. gate that kept her inside, and it swung right open.

"Well, that was easy!" Roxy yipped with joy and started to walk out.

"Roxy!" Velvet meowed fiercely from her deck. "You can't leave! Someone might take you!"

"I just want to have some fun! Come on, and follow me. I know you can do it." Roxy encouraged as she strolled away.

Velvet couldn't let her best friend leave on her own, she thought nervously. She had to go with Roxy and make sure she was safe, but she was just so scared!

Velvet watched as Roxy trotted further away.
She decided she needed to go with her friend.

"Hey, wait for me! Don't leave me behind."
Velvet wailed.

Roxy's ears perked up as she looked behind her.
"I knew you would come!" she cheered. "Where
should we go first?"

"I don't know. I never leave my hou
Where do you go on your walks wit
your owner?" Roxy suddenly stoppe
and got all excited.

"I know exactly where to go!"

"Where are we?" Velvet asked when they stopped walking.

"It's a mini-golf course!" Roxy said lovingly while her head followed the balls back and forth.

"Let's go in," Roxy said excitedly. Velvet trailed behind with her tail between her legs.

Velvet sat in the bushes while she watched Roxy run around and have fun. She wondered why she decided to follow Roxy.

Roxy found Velvet hiding in a bush and gently pushed a ball towards her. "Come on, play with me. You'll get belly rubs from humans if you do!"

Oooooooo!

AAYYYAAAY!

"I feel much better in here," Velvet's voice quivered from her curled up position deep in a bush.

"Fine, let's go find someplace quieter." Velvet nodded in agreement and darted out after Roxy.

Velvet followed Roxy closely down the street, still shaken from the mini-golf scene. Velvet was not enjoying this outing.

Roxy took her into the busiest part of town, and Velvet was dodging people left and right. 'Where on Earth was this crazy canine taking me?' Velvet thought to herself.

"What are we doing here?" Velvet
questioned.

"Have you ever had ice cream!?" Roxy blurted
excitedly. Velvet let out an animated meow, ice
cream was her favorite treat!

Roxy walked confidently around the groups of people lined up outside, and plopped down next to two mini-humans messily eating their ice cream.

"Puppy!" One of them screeched. The other mini-human laughed joyfully and bent down to pet Velvet.

"Here, kitty, have some ice cream," the mini-human said, holding her cone out to Velvet.

Velvet took a careful lick and started to purr because she was so happy.

Roxy looked up at the other mini-human with puppy dog eyes, and she finally got some ice cream too!

With full bellies, Velvet and Roxy found a shady spot to relax.

"Now where do you want to go?" Roxy asked from their spot under a tree.

"I've always wanted to go to the beach," Velvet admitted.

Roxy picked her head up and began to protest, "No, let's find somewhere else to go."

"Why not? It sounds like a good time." Velvet said standing up, starting to walk away.

"Because I'm scared," Roxy admitted shyly.

"What? Why are you scared?" Velvet inquired.

"Be...be...because there's so much water there, and I...I...I don't like water."

"Roxy, all day I was so scared to leave my house because I hadn't done it before, but you encouraged me to do it. This new experience has changed my life. Now, it's my turn to push you. I believe in you." Velvet said in a comforting tone.

As much as she didn't want to, Roxy sheepishly trailed behind Velvet the whole walk to the beach. When they got to the beach, Roxy immediately stopped.

"I'll j...j...just wait right here while y...y...you explore the beach." She said while planting herself on the boardwalk.

"No, we're in this together." Velvet said firmly.

With a little nudge from Velvet, Roxy nervously made her way to the beach but refused to go down to the water. She was enjoying the sand just fine.

When the water touched Velvet's paws, she finally felt relaxed.

Velvet called to Roxy, begging her to just try and touch the water, "Get your paws wet! It feels so good!."

"No way!" Roxy proclaimed. But, after a little persuading, she walked carefully to the water with Velvet right by her side.

When the first wave ran over Roxy's paws, she yelped and ran away. "Try again Roxy, you're doing great!" Velvet reassured.

Roxy tried again. "It's not as scary as I thought it would be," she said.

"I prefer running through the sprinkler over the ocean though."

"That's alright," Velvet said. "The most important thing is that you tried."

They began to play as Roxy got more comfortable. When the sun began to set, and the air became cooler Velvet said with a shiver, "Roxy, I think we stayed out too long."

"I think it's time to go home," Roxy said in agreement.

Together, they ran home with wagging tails.

As they neared their homes, they saw their owners standing outside worried.

"I was so worried about you. Where did you go?" Velvet's owner said.

"Don't you ever open the fence again. You could have gotten lost!" said Roxy's owner.

From her owner's arms, Velvet purred, "Goodnight Roxy. I had a lot of fun today."

"Goodnight Velvet, thanks for always being there for me," Roxy exclaimed!

When Velvet was back inside her house, she realized that the outside world wasn't so scary, and as long as she had her friend by her side, she could do anything.

9 781087 957678